A MESSAGE TO PARENTS

Reading good books to young children is a crucial factor in a child's psychological and intellectual development. It promotes a mutually warm and satisfying relationship between parent and child and enhances the child's awareness of the world around him. It stimulates the child's imagination and lays a foundation for the development of the skills necessary to support the critical thinking process. In addition, the parent who reads to his child helps him to build vocabulary and other prerequisite skills for the child's own successful reading.

In order to provide parents and children with books which will do these things, Brown Watson has published this series of small books specially designed for young children. These books are factual, fanciful, humorous, questioning and adventurous. A library acquired in this inexpensive way will provide many hours of pleasurable and profitable reading for parents and children.

Published by Brown Watson (Leicester) Ltd.
ENGLAND
© 1980 Rand McNally & Company
Printed and bound in the German Democratic Republic.

Little Boy Blue's
HORN

By HELEN WING

Illustrated by IRMA WILDE

Brown Watson

England.

Little Boy Blue
    Come blow your horn,
The sheep's in the meadow,
    The cow's in the corn.
Where's the little boy
    Who looks after the sheep?
Under the haystack, fast asleep.
When he woke from his nap
    Boy Blue looked around,
There wasn't a cow or a sheep
    To be found.

He dashed through a field
    Where the corn was so tall
That Little Boy Blue could see
    Nothing at all.

When he pushed his way out
    At the end of the field
He met a fat piggy
    Who grunted and squealed.

"Please help me, kind Piggy,"
  Said Little Boy Blue,
"I've lost a brown cow
  And a woolly sheep, too."

"I'm glad that you asked me,"
    Said Piggy with pride.
"Just toot on your horn
    And I'll trot at your side."

They went down a road
    Winding this way and that,
When who should they meet
    But a talkative cat!

"I am handsome and clever,"
   Said Cat, "and you'll see
As we travel along
   I'll be good company."

At the side of the road
A little white hen
Was scratching up gravel
Outside her pen.
She said to Boy Blue
With a cluckity-cluck,
"If you'll take me along
I'll bring you good luck.

"I'm a clever hen
    Though I'm not very big,
And if I get tired
    I can ride on the pig."

Boy Blue took his horn
    And tooted some more
When they came to a house
    With a tumble-down door.

They peeked through the cracks
Of the rickety house
But no one was home
But a squeakity mouse.

"We're hunting a cow
        And a sheep," said Boy Blue,
"Squeak-squeak," said the mouse,
        "I will come along, too.

"I've been a shy mouse
    Since the day I was born,
So if Cat chases me
    I'll ride in your horn."

When they came to a river,
They climbed in a boat,
Then they pulled up the anchor
And started to float.

They looked to the left
    And they looked to the right
But never a cow or a sheep
    Came in sight.

The boat started leaking
    And bounced up and down
So they waded ashore
    At the very next town.

They went to a shop
  And bought strawberry pop
And ginger-snap biscuits
  With icing on top.

Little Boy Blue said,
   "We mustn't delay
Or I won't find my sheep
   Or my brown cow today."

They were searching the woods
When a dog with a yelp
Said, "If you're in trouble
Perhaps I can help.

"I'll sniff with my nose
        And we'll follow the scent
Till we come to the place
        Where your animals went."

Boy Blue was so happy
   He shouted with joy
And tooted his horn
   Like a new Christmas toy,

When he saw in a farmyard
Just over the way,
His cow and his sheep
Fast asleep in the hay.